Scene

Brandy

A. Ryan Nerz

Aladdin Paperbacks

FOR TINA

First Aladdin Paperbacks edition February 1999

Cover photo: ©1998 by Larry Ford/Outline

Text copyright ©1999 by 17th Street Productions Threads page by Stacie Amador

Produced by 17th Street Productions, a division of Daniel Weiss Associates, Inc. 33 West 17th Street New York, NY 10011

Aladdin Paperbacks An imprint of Simon & Schuster Children's Publishing Division 1230 Avenue of the Americas New York, NY 10020

Designed by Michael Rivilis Printed and bound in the United States of America 10 9 8 7 6 5 4 3 2 1

Library of Congress Catalog Card Number 98-73800 ISBN: 0-689-82545-5

Sittin' on

Brandy with her brother, Ray J.

Top of the World

Brandy is living proof that you can become a huge star . . . by just sittin' around.

She was just a seven-year-old sittin' up in her room, watching Whitney Houston on MTV, when she realized her calling. Eight years later she was already sittin' in a comfy chair . . . at the Grammy awards, hoping to score some hardware for her quad-platinum debut album. And she was just sittin' next to Whitney Houston in a jeweled carriage when sixty million TV viewers watched her as the first black Cinderella. Even now, Brandy will admit that with a second megahit album, her own hugely popular sitcom, and a starring role in a Hollywood movie, she's just "Sittin' on Top of the World."

But don't let all the sitting fool you. She's also pretty good at standing. Just ask Little Richard, who witnessed Brandy's first public performance.

In 1985 Little Richard and Bo Diddley gave a huge concert at the Los Angeles Forum. Brandy's mother, Sonja Norwood, is Diddley's cousin, so Sonja decided to take her six-year-old daughter to the show. When Little Richard finished his set, he invited the audience to come up and sing a tune with him. Gangly, doe-eyed Brandy rushed the stage and stood front and center, basking in the spotlight. She sang along, belting out each lyric with emotion. When the song ended to a roaring crowd, she beamed and bowed. Afterward she admitted to her mom, "For a minute, I thought that was my audience."

Think maybe she has performing in her blood?

Apparently. When Brandy was born on February 11, 1979, in McComb, Mississippi, Sonja Norwood already knew what was up. "I told the doctor, 'I have just given birth to a star.' I knew she was going to be somebody one day."

And Brandy must have agreed because she hit the ground singing.

© Gary Gershoff/Retna Ltd.

Performing at the urbanAID 4 LIFEbeat at Madison Square Garden.

Her mom remembers, "When she was a baby, my mom would hold her for hours and sing to her. Brandy grew up singing. She could sing before she could talk."

Soon singing wasn't enough. Brandy needed an audience. At age two she sang her first solo in church in Brookhaven, Mississippi. With that experience behind her, Brandy took the show on the road . . . to her bedroom, where she performed, with microphone, for a patient audience of dolls.

By age four Brandy's talent and stage thirst were undeniable. The family packed up and moved to Carson, California, near Los Angeles. She immediately began the flurry of auditions, tryouts, and talent shows that young star wanna-bes must endure. At twelve she sang backup vocals for the R&B

Brandy sang at the opening of the Goodwill Games in New York in July 1998, and she cohosted the Lady of Soul Awards in September 1998.

group Immature. Finally Brandy met a producer who began shopping her to various record labels.

Why did Ron Shapiro, the executive vice president of Atlantic Records, decide to risk his neck and sign a fourteen-year-old unknown? Well, her angelic voice didn't hurt, but the deciding factor was her spunk. At an industry showcase, where entertainment bigwigs got together for a private little concert, Brandy demanded respect. Ron remembers: "It was a big, jaded crowd, and when she started singing, they started talking. And she just stopped singing. She said, 'You're being rude.' And I panicked. And the crowd silenced. But then she started singing, and they listened. And she won them over."

And just like that, Brandy was on her way to becoming somebody.

Brandy gets her hair braided with synthetic hair extensions every three weeks. It takes around eight or nine hours!

At the tenth annual *Soul Train* Music Awards in 1996.

Little Ole

So it'd be tough to claim that Brandy's a "regular girl."

You know, since she's a teenage superstar and all.

But she swears it's true.

And really, beneath the whole superstar thing, Brandy Rayana Norwood does seem pretty normal. She fights with Mom about her outfits and begs "Dadda" to extend her curfew. She was picked on in elementary and junior high school for being skinny and unattractive. ("I guess I was just pickable," she says.) She loves movies and Polo Sport clothes and only eats at McDonald's and Sizzler.

That all sounds normal. But she's gotta live in a mansion, right?

Nope. The Norwood clan lives in a four-bedroom house on a quiet, middle-class street in Los Angeles. And that's after they became millionaires. Until recently they still lived in their modest home in Carson, the town next to Compton, the rough home base of gangsta rap.

So Brandy doesn't live in a mansion, and she is not spoiled. Her family is ultratight, and her parents trained her to be a hardworking, considerate, God-fearing lady. Sonja Norwood, who is Brandy's manager, was dead serious about raising healthy kids. "You have to decide what kind of kids you want. We don't believe in sparing the rod. If they did something wrong, they got spanked. My kids have always been very respectable, polite, and well mannered."

Accordingly, Sonja is fiercely protective of Brandy's image. Producers and agents have learned to both fear and respect

Mrs. Norwood, who is always by her daughter's side. Mrs. Norwood is acutely aware of Tinsel Town's tendency to eat its young alive, and she simply won't have it: "No one, no one is going to have the opportunity of taking the principles that we've instilled in my child and shape her into somebody else." That's why, until very recently, Brandy had never cursed, never had a make-out session, and never showed her navel on-screen. (She broke all these rules in the movie *I Still Know What You Did Last Summer*.) At one point Brandy swore she wouldn't show her navel until "fans start writing, 'Brandy, we're ready to see your navel.'"

Imagine deciding not to show your belly button for business reasons! Well, that's the not-so-normal part of Brandy's childhood.

It's also not all that normal to go to the prom with NBA sensation Kobe Bryant. Touted by some as the next Michael Jordan (for his ability and looks), Kobe was a lesser-known high school standout when he met Brandy at the Essence Awards in New York City. Kobe was so taken by Brandy that he immediately asked her to his Lower Merion High School prom in Pennsylvania. She was psyched, but she didn't reply until four days later after okaying it with Mom. This shows just how carefully Brandy maintains her image: "I'm safe. Sometimes too safe. I want every move I make to be right. Like, I thought it was a good idea for me to go to the prom with Kobe Bryant. He's a guy with a good image, comes from a good family."

Come prom time, Brandy arrived in Philadelphia with a full entourage—her makeup artist,

Brandy with Kobe Bryant at his prom in 1996.

her hairstylist, her bodyguard, and her mother. On May 24, 1996, the night before the prom, she had her first official date—she went with Kobe to Atlantic City to see a concert by love songster Barry White. Prom night snapshots show Brandy aglow, hair swept up, wearing a shimmering gold cape and gown. Kobe must have made quite an impression, judging from Brandy's remarks. "I've never been treated like that by anyone before. Kobe made me feel beautiful." She later said, "I would marry a guy like Kobe Bryant. I would marry Kobe today." What a fairy tale that would be.

Despite her claim to be your basic, run-of-the-mill gal, Brandy simply cannot pull it off. Her sixteenth, seventeenth, and eighteenth birthday parties were star-studded bashes at the Hard Rock Café, Planet Hollywood, and Hollywood's House of Blues, respectively. She had a weekly allowance of a thousand dollars. Mariah Carey sent her private jet for Brandy's convenient travel to the *Billboard* Awards. It's not too bold to say that she's blown her cover with the normal crowd.

Brandy's seventeen-year-old brother hasn't exactly taken the normal route, either. Like his big sis, Ray J. has already made music

If Brandy ever does move away from home, she says she'd probably head east to *New York City*. She loves dressing up in fly outfits and hitting the *New York* hot spots with hipsters and hip-hoppers.

and appeared in TV and movies. In 1997 he released his own debut album, *Everything You Want*, with Elektra Records and has since signed with Brandy's label, Atlantic.

Though Ray J.'s a bit lower on the stardom totem pole than Brandy, she'll tell you that he's too busy being a sweetheart brother to be jealous: "He's my heart . . . because he doesn't tell my mom about every little bad thing I do. But seriously, we hang out and talk about everything. I can even talk to him about guys, although sometimes he'll say, 'Brandy, I really don't wanna talk about that stuff. Don't go there.'" Unfortunately for Brandy, Ray J. plans on moving out when he turns eighteen, leaving her one less shoulder to cry on. "That hurts me more than anything, that he's gonna be gone, you know. He's my confidant. When I cry, I go to him because he listens to me."

Dad Willie Norwood has been listening to both of them for years. Before they hit the big time, Ray J. and Brandy performed every Sunday in the front row of the Los Angeles Avalon Church of Christ, where their father is still minister of music. A soft-spoken man and a talented musician, Willie Norwood is in charge of all musical aspects of his kids' careers, but he humbly downplays his influence: "I taught Brandy and Ray J. how to appreciate singing. I wouldn't say I taught them how to sing, because they already knew that, but I taught them through interaction how to do it better."

There you have it—the well-oiled machine that is The Norwood Family. Pops handles the music, Moms handles the business, and the kids, well, they're stars.

Threads

Want to get this look?

When you think of Brandy, those fabulous braids come to mind, and we've found out what Brandy uses to keep her braids full of luster and shine.

*   Aveda Essential Oils for treatments
*   Let's Jam! for hold
*   Optimum Oil for luster
*   A satin scarf at night to maintain the look even longer

Brandy is fresh and trendy with her . . .
<u>TIE-DYED COTTON CAMISOLE</u>

Wanna make your own tie-dyed cami? Here's how:

*   One cami (any material)
*   Any color Rit dye
*   String or rubber bands

1. Take the cami and twist it, knot it, or just gather it up in separate sections. Secure tightly with the string.
2. Follow "How to dye" directions on the back of the bottle.
3. Let dry, cut off string, and you've created your own cool cami!

Other totally trendy tie-dyed threads we've seen Brandy wearing around town:

*   Slip
*   Sundress
*   Khakis
*   Cardigan

The look is

<u>ULTRASLIM HIP HUGGERS</u>

<u>STRAPPY PLATFORM SANDALS</u>

And, of course, the most versatile, important, and trendy accessory for the summer, A CARDIGAN

Summertime Cool

Brandy's Filmography

I Still Know What You Did Last Summer (1998)
Cinderella (1997) TV movie
Moesha (1996–?) TV series
Thea (1993) TV series
Arachnophobia (1990)

Brandy's Discography

Never Say Never (1998)
"Missing You," *from Set It Off sound track* (1996)
"Sittin' Up In My Room," *from Waiting to Exhale sound track* (1996)
"Where Are You Now," *from Batman Forever sound track* (1995)
Brandy (1994)

Blowin'

Brandy proudly displays her MTV Movie Award in 1996.

Up

At fourteen, it's tough to get all your phone calls done in the evening. But to record an album on top of phone calls?

Well, Brandy found a way to fit it all in. But who could have predicted that this little girl's first album was gonna be so large? Its first release, "I Wanna Be Down," spread Brandy's honey vocals on some light hip-hop toast, and American listeners ate it up. It soared to number one on the R&B charts and was top three on the pop charts. The beat on her second single, "Baby," was so catchy, so funky, that it really only needed one lyric—the word baby. There's something about the way Brandy sings it—sassy, smooth, and seductive—that the single word just never sounds tired. The song went platinum, another top-three hit on the pop charts. Her other release, "Brokenhearted," was top ten with gold status.

Brandy was an instant star. By the age of fifteen she had sold four million albums! Add a couple of Grammy nominations, an American Music Award, and four *Soul Train* Music Awards (she beat out Janet Jackson), and Brandy's no longer a cute little girl with braids. She's history book material.

But Brandy wasn't quite done yet. She made a remix of "I Wanna Be Down" with some of the big girls—Queen Latifah, MC Lyte, and Yo Yo—which rose to number five. Then Brandy recorded "Sittin' Up in My Room" for the *Waiting to Exhale* sound track. It eventually sold a million copies, while Brandy's video wallpapered MTV.

Though she hardly needed it at the time, Brandy did a nationwide high school tour to increase her first album's word-of-mouth popularity. Soon after she opened for R&B quartet Boyz II Men on their 1995 North American tour, Wanya Morris, who was a tenor in the band and an established pop star, took an instant liking to Brandy—in a somewhat brotherly way. But Wanya's voice made Brandy swoon, and she had a big ole crush on him. "He was my favorite because his vocal runs are out of the ordinary. But he didn't like me. I was fifteen years old—what did he want to do with me?"

Even if he had wanted to do something with Brandy, her mom wasn't having it. Sonja promised "Boyz II Men would become a trio" if Wanya asked Brandy out before she turned eighteen. So he waited until the big eighteen and then asked her out.

Wanya was Brandy's first love, and she fell hard. Her affections for him had been piling up for some time. She had certainly been charmed when he and the Boyz sang "Happy Birthday" a cappella for her at her sweet sixteen. Afterward they gave her a diamond tennis bracelet, gold heart-shaped earrings with diamonds, and a matching pendant. Brandy swooned and held back the tears.

They were an all-smiles couple for over a year despite busy schedules and long periods apart from each other. In the February 1998 issue of *Ebony*, Brandy and Wanya were named one of the magazine's "10 Hottest Couples" along with such power pairs as Will Smith and Jada Pinkett. Unfortunately, though, by the time the article came out, Wanya had already broken Brandy's heart. In her words, they split "because he's so busy and I'm so busy."

Brandy's been coping with the breakup ever since, sad but strong: "I was sick, and it was hard, really hard, but I got through it. I'm okay now. I miss him, but I'm okay. He's special to me. But we had to move on. . . . Whoever he ends up with will be happy."

She can rest assured of one thing—there will be many applicants for her empty boyfriend slot.

Laughing it up as "Mo."

Mo' Better

Brandy will surely take her place among the elite One Name Club—Prince (The Artist). Tupac. Janet. Leo. Madonna. And Brandy. But Brandy has the opportunity to create an even more select group—the Two One-Name Club. Because she's not just Brandy. She's Moesha, too.

The similarities between Brandy and her on-screen character are scary. Even Brandy thinks so. "Brandy kind of matched Moesha," Brandy says. "Her attitude is the same. She's interested in boys, but something else comes first—her schoolwork, her family. She hangs out with her friends. She's very nice. . . . Really, I'm nice to everybody. I'm, like, 'Hi, my name is Brandy.' And I'll give people a hug. I'll go up to people and say things like, 'I like your hair.' Stuff like that. Moesha is the same way."

These similarities made casting the star role a no-brainer for Moesha producers. After Brandy's stirring audition they decided to change the character's age from the originally scripted fourteen to make her closer to Brandy's age. "We just sat down and talked to her. She was so genuine. She said, 'I am Moesha.' As soon as she said it, we knew it was true."

© Everett Collection

The cast of *Thea*.

19

As a sixteen-year-old with only one prior role (as Danesha on the short-lived 1993–94 sitcom *Thea*), Brandy walked into a room of TV executives who had gathered to see if she was worthy of star status. She sensed their nervousness and said, "Now, guys, don't worry. This is your show. If you put it on TV, I guarantee a hit."

And what a hit it has been. Now in its fourth season, *Moesha* is UPN's top-rated show (besides *Star Trek: Voyager,* of course). It's hip enough to attract droves of urban teenagers yet clean-cut enough to win the 1996 Parents' Choice Silver Honor. Moesha's not corny or preachy. The characters speak ghetto slang, but they're not trying too hard to be "down." According to rapper Busta Rhymes, *Moesha* is simply "the phattest show out there."

For such a phat show, *Moesha* has a pretty simple concept. Moesha Mitchell is your basic teenager dealing with your basic teenage problems. The show's drama centers around friends and family, not gangs and trauma. At Moesha's sixteenth birthday party a guest is patted down for a gun, but nobody ever pulls one. Most of the time Moesha and her crew just hang at a coffee shop called The Den. Mo chills with her best friends,

"I like affection . . . I like a person to stand up for what he wants and for himself. Don't let me run over you. . . ."

The cast of *Moesha.*

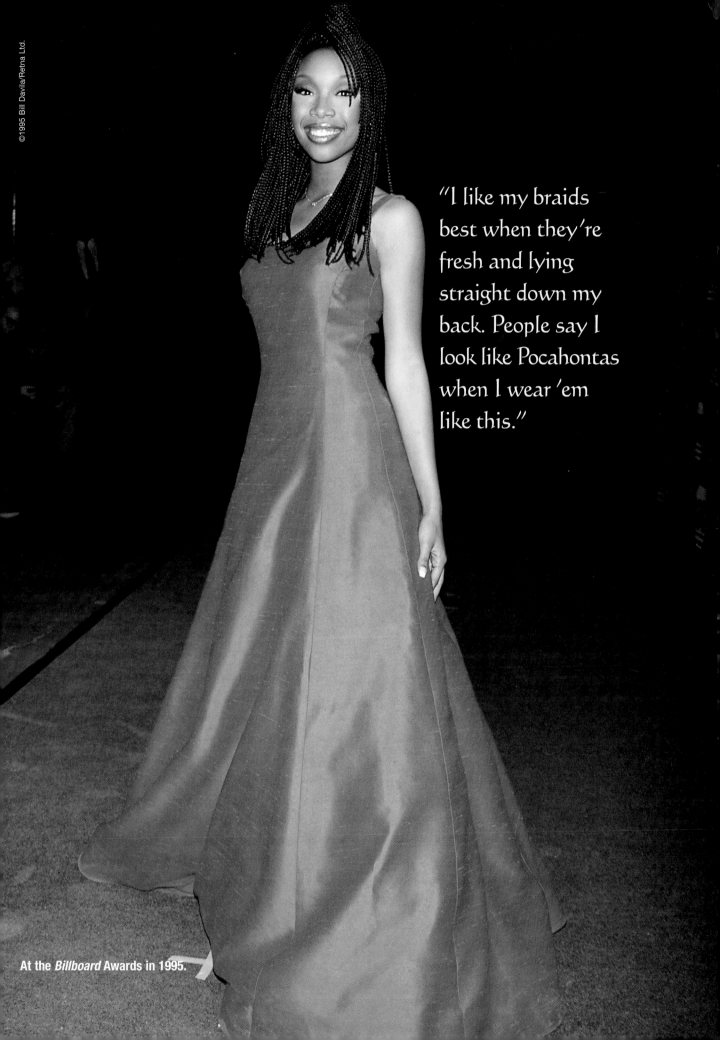

"I like my braids best when they're fresh and lying straight down my back. People say I look like Pocahontas when I wear 'em like this."

At the *Billboard* Awards in 1995.

boy-crazy Kim and Niecy, and next-door-neighbor guy pal Hakeem. The kids just bust on each other and drop one-liners like Kim's signature, "He's *foiiine!*" Moesha's biggest trauma is that she received a new Saturn instead of the Jeep she wanted.

In between takes, the set of *Moesha* is one big party and the studio audience is invited! Teens of all different ethnicities have little talent contests in the stands, and they rush to grab autographs from the cast after taping. A DJ spins hip-hop and R&B while both cast and crowd dance.

Not a bad situation for a girl who once almost gave up on acting. After her mediocre stint on *Thea,* Brandy had written her acting career off entirely. "I was a singer, and I didn't want to act. I read the script for *Moesha,* and they said it was mine. Now I like doing it all."

Despite her apparent confidence, though, she still rates her acting as a lowly one on a scale of ten.

But fans disagree, and producers are astounded at Brandy's improvement. Sara Finney, one of *Moesha's* executive producers, says, "She can

knows how good she is as Moesha. She has a natural ability that just stuns you. She lights up the screen as soon as she comes out."

With such stage presence and a go-getter attitude, Brandy should be lighting up screens for a while.

"I've always wanted to be a cheerleader and all that stuff. At least with Moesha, I can have a little glimpse of what being in high school is like."

carry scenes, and anything we give her, she does it. She really digs deep. Even though we are a comedy, we sometimes get into some real issues, and she can pull it off." Vida Spears, another producer, says, "Sometimes I don't think she

"I want to keep challenging myself in the world of show business. Everything that's hard, I want to do. I'm my own toughest critic. I'm really hard on myself, and that's the way you have to be."

You go, girl.

On the set of *Moesha*.

Cind

Brandy with her fairy godmother, Whitney.

erella Story

Brandy may not really be Cinderella, but they have the same fairy godmother.

When Whitney Houston handpicked Brandy to play the title role in *Rodgers & Hammerstein's Cinderella,* she knew what she was doing: "Brandy's perfect. She has the energy, the verve, the eyes, the wonder. And our relationship comes off really well on the screen because it starts from real life."

So the same woman who unknowingly sparked Brandy's singing ambitions later knowingly chose her to become the first black Cinderella. And that's before the fairy tale even begins. . . .

Originally Whitney was supposed to play Cinderella. But the first project of Houston's BrownHouse Productions was delayed a few years and, as a thirty-three-year-old mother, Whitney felt too old.

She called Brandy, apparently just to say hello. Brandy remembers vividly, "She was telling me about Bobbi Kris [Whitney's five-year-old daughter], and then all of a sudden she says, 'I'm doing *Cinderella.*' I asked, 'Can I play one of your evil stepsisters, please, please?' She said, "No, I want you to play Cinderella.'"

Brandy thanked Nippy (her nickname for Whitney) repeatedly, then dropped the phone and ran to her mother, screaming. "It's a fairy tale, really. I'm waiting for someone to pinch me," Brandy said.

No need to pinch her, though, because this was the real deal, complete with marble staircase, elegant wedding gown, and most importantly, a handsome prince. It would be the same classic tale. Poor, beautiful Cinderella scrubs floors for her snotty sisters and evil stepmother. Fairy godmother gives Cinderella a makeover and a pumpkin vehicle so she can go to the Prince's ball. At the ball Prince and Cinderella cut a rug and fall in love, just in time for Cinderella to lose her makeover and pumpkinmobile. Prince then schlepps around countryside with glass slipper and finally finds Cinderella. Based on her great feet, dancing ability, and the all-important "love at first sight," Prince marries Cinderella.

So why not just rerelease the original Julie Andrews version of *Cinderella*? Because it's the nineties, baby! It needed a multiracial cast to fit the times. In the words of Whoopi Goldberg, who played the queen, "Before, it was either all-black or all-white.

The cast of *Cinderella*.

But never a normal mix of people. This integrated cast is how the real world is. This is how I live."

In addition to Whitney, Brandy, and Whoopi, *Cinderella* starred another African American actress, Natalie Desselle (who appeared with Halle Berry in *B.A.P.S.*), as the itchy stepsister, Minerva. Veanne Cox played Calliope, the other stepsister; Victor Garber was King Maximilian; and Jason Alexander, who was George on *Seinfeld*, played Lionel, the prince's valet.

For the opportunity to play opposite Brandy as the prince, over three hundred young studs auditioned. Producers chose a handsome twenty-four-year-old Filipino, Paolo Montalban. He remembers when he first met

Brandy: "The first thing she said was, 'I'm Brandy and I'm eighteen. What's your name and how old are you?' It was like a first date—with twelve chaperons scrutinizing your every move . . . and a camera."

Once the cameras started rolling, Brandy discovered that *Cinderella* would take more work than *Moesha*. Whereas each thirty-minute episode of *Moesha* was shot within a week, entire days were dedicated to shooting one

With Whoopi Goldberg at the *Cinderella* premiere in Los Angeles.

five-minute scene of *Cinderella*. And, of course, there was the matter of de-Brandifying her voice for the purposes of a musical. This required a singing coach, who showed Brandy how to act out her singing and enunciate each word clearly. She had to learn, rather quickly, to drop the drawn-out R&B riffs like "Baby, baby, baaaabaay!" in favor of crisp, perfect speech.

It wasn't all work on the set, though. Whoopi and Jason Alexander filled the downtime with jokes, and Whitney and Brandy chased each other around the studio lot on electric golf carts. Other stars stopped by, like Angela Bassett, who visited Whoopi on the last day of shooting. Brandy, who is generally starstruck, was especially bowled over by Bassett's cameo. Brandy ran up and gave her a hug, showering her with compliments and offers: "What are you doing here? When can we be in a movie together? I'll do anything. I can cry. I'll do whatever. . . ."

Judging from *Cinderella*'s staggeringly high ratings, Brandy might just get her chance to play alongside Bassett. With sixty million viewers, *Cinderella* was ABC's highest-rated special in thirteen years! The attraction of the Cinderella story had never been in doubt, but some had wondered whether the multicultural approach and high budget would lead to failure. But in the end, it all paid off.

As for Brandy's career, *Cinderella* certainly was no setback. It not only confirmed the popularity of her singing but also showed she had the stuff to hit the big screen. But perhaps most importantly, in a business where timing and luck mean everything, Brandy proved once again that she has the Midas touch. All that she touches turns to gold . . . or platinum.

"She doesn't want me to commit to anybody. She wants me to just be young and to know what I want in a guy."
—Brandy on Whitney Houston

© Everett Collection

Cinderella finds her prince.

Ne

"I'm not, like, a mad female that has a lot of anger—this is not my <u>Control</u> album [by Janet Jackson]. I'm just me. It's about what I would do to make my life better with a loved one."

Performing at the *Soul Train* Music Awards in 1996.

ver Say Never

Considering that all Brandy had known in her short life was absurdly good luck, you'd think she wouldn't worry about her second album, <u>Never Say Never</u>.

But as the countdown to its release date (June 9, 1998) began, Brandy was noticeably worried. "Your second album is supposed to do better than your first one. So I'm a little scared."

Her producers weren't scared, though. Robert Shapiro of Atlantic Records said, "It's part of her charm. She hasn't missed yet, but she's always calling me in a sweet little voice, saying, 'Do you think it's [the album] going to be okay?'"

And, as expected, it was more than okay. Realizing she had to deliver more maturity on her sophomore album, Brandy was up to the task: "You know, this is not like 'Sittin' Up in My Room' because I was sixteen then, and I did sit up in my room talkin' about, 'Oh, God, what's Wanya doin'?' Now I'm nineteen. And it's like, 'You know what? You're going to respect me.'" Now, after experiencing some growing pains—most notably breaking up with Wanya—she feels her second album is "deeper" and "more emotionally there."

That means no more schoolgirl crushes and no more wanting to be "down." Through her lyrics we find she's grown up and kicked an undeserving boyfriend out the door. She's found the strength to overcome a broken heart. And her signature raspy voice, though still sweet, has matured into that of a woman. Filled with simmering grooves, funky guitar loops, and hip-hop beats, *Never Say Never* is Brandy's giant musical step toward adulthood. In the words of a *USA Today* reviewer, who gave the CD three and a half stars out of four, "She's grown up, but she's still Brandy."

Even before the album debuted, it's first release—her surprise duet with Monica, "The Boy Is Mine,"—had already topped the pop and R&B charts. The song had received some press before its release because of the common assumption that Brandy and Monica were archenemies. Wrong.

When Brandy called Monica in Atlanta, Monica couldn't believe that it was actually her. Brandy

Brandy with Wanya Morris at the *Cinderella* premiere in New York City.

remembers the conversation perfectly: "She was like, 'Stop playing, man. It's too early. Don't be callin' me saying you're Brandy. Sing something.'" After Brandy proved her identity, she told Monica she wanted to do a duet. "'Cause I mean, you know how people talk about us and try to put us against each other. We should just go out and shock 'em."

The next week Brandy flew to Atlanta to record "The Boy Is Mine," a sassy vocal argument over a boy, who, in the end, gets dissed by both divas. Between recording sessions Brandy and Monica had a great time hitting the town together. They went shopping, chatted about the biz, and even hit the Magic Mountain theme park. When recording ended, Monica was so satisfied with the tune that she made it the title track for her sophomore album, released just a month after Brandy's.

The video, featuring hottie Mekhi Phifer (*Clockers*) as "The Boy," was just as popular as the song. It was nominated for the 1998 MTV Video Music Awards in two categories—Video of the Year and Best R&B Video.

Never Say Never's second release, "Top of the World," features the handsome upstart Bad Boy rapper, Mase. With its head-bobbin' hip-hop backbeat and Brandy's buttery chorus, "Top of the World" bumps from the ghettos to the suburbs. Brandy sings about the myth that celebrity changes people and how "a little dough" can't erase her problems. Interestingly, Mase's rap, which boasts that he bought his mom a Benz and has "enough dough to buy the town," seems to say the opposite. Still, Mase's monotone

rap fits perfectly with Brandy's sugary singing, and the song feels like a celebration.

Their duet must have convinced the world of their compatibility because the rumors flew that Brandy and Mase were an item. Tabloids spotted Brandy kissing Mase after a brawl at a New York party thrown by Puff Daddy. *Vibe* magazine ran a blurb saying that they were a couple and that Brandy's mom, who is also Mase's manager, was "pleased as punch." Brandy doesn't deny that she "comforted" Mase after the Puff party incident, but she swears they've never been an item (notice the stuttering, though): "He's not my type. I like those kind of guys that . . . hmmm. I don't know. Mase is my friend. What is the world coming to? I don't have a boyfriend. I'm so single right now. It's better that way. Guys are . . . Mase probably has millions of women."

That doesn't sound much like the girl who sat up in her room, daydreaming about Wanya. Perhaps that's because in her personal relationships, in her music, and on the screen, Brandy has matured before our very eyes.

Brandy's quick maturation is no surprise, though, considering all she's accomplished. But she still hadn't become a movie star . . . yet.

Before 1998, Brandy only had one big screen role, as an eleven-year-old in the 1990 spider flick, *Arachnophobia*. And the part was small—almost microscopic.

But now Brandy is cashing in on the teen horror trend. She stars alongside Jennifer Love Hewitt and Mekhi Phifer in *I Still Know What You Did Last Summer*, the sequel to 1997's slasher smash, *I*

With Mariah Carey at the *Billboard* Music Awards in 1996.

Know What You Did Last Summer. Brandy plays a kick-boxing, party-girl waitress who wins, along with her college roommate (Hewitt), a free trip to the Bahamas. Everything's cool—good times on the beach with roomie and boyfriend (Phifer)—until that menacing rain-slickered killer starts hacking away. The movie allows Brandy to show off some new acting skills: "I get to show people that I'm really scared. I have to react to things. I have to show different sides of my personality."

That's not the only thing Brandy shows off. *I Still Know* marks her first on-screen curse word and the first public unveiling of the bod (she sports a bikini), which her mother/manager has kept stubbornly under wraps throughout her teen screen years.

The bikini thing is no big deal in itself except that it marks Brandy's increasing independence from her parents. The ten-week *I Still Know* shoot near Tenacatita, Mexico, was Brandy's longest stint away from Mom . . . ever. At first Brandy wanted her mom to come, but Sonja Norwood said she was too busy. Brandy remembers her reaction: "I said, 'No! I want you to come.' But when I got here, I thought, 'I'm cool. I'm chillin'. So I'm kinda glad she's busy. She doesn't have to worry about me. I'm a grown-up person." Indeed she is.

That's why she wants her movie career to steer toward more grown-up roles. "I want just one *Bodyguard* movie! I want more of a challenge. I don't want the role of a regular teenager. I would love to play a role where I'm a person in control of everything, a challenging role. I have played the innocent roles: *Moesha* is innocent; *Cinderella* was innocent."

With all that she has accomplished by the ripe age of nineteen, Brandy Norwood can hardly be considered innocent. She's knee-deep in three mediums—television, music, and film. She's a runway model in Milan and a college student in Malibu (at Pepperdine University). She has a print-ad campaign with Candie's shoes and a DC Comics book character! But she wants more—like, say, her own beauty salon and record company. You see, she's not worried about fatigue; she's worried about missing out: "If I don't work, I'm afraid I'll miss something. I love to work. I want a star on Hollywood Boulevard. I want all of it. I want to win a Grammy. I've been nominated five times. Don't you think I deserve one?"

Wouldn't want her to miss out.

The Low-down on Brandy

Full name: Brandy Rayana Norwood **Birthplace:** McComb, Mississippi **Birth date:** February 11, 1979 **Astrological sign:** Aquarius **Height:** 5'7" **Weight:** 115 lbs. **Shoe size:** 7 **Size of her glass slipper in** *Cinderella:* 5 **Pets:** Dogs Labby and Feather **Favorite singers:** Whitney Houston, Boyz II Men, Mase, Puff Daddy, Notorious B.I.G., Erykah Badu, Mariah Carey, and Celine Dion **Favorite actor:** Larenz Tate **Favorite actress:** Angela Bassett **Favorite TV shows:** *Roseanne, Home Improvement, Family Matters,* and *The Parent 'Hood* **Favorite female supermodels:** Tyra Banks, Naomi Campbell, and Veronica Webb **Favorite male supermodel:** Tyson Beckford **Favorite designers:** Todd Oldham, Tommy Hilfiger, Donna Karan, Dolce & Gabbana **Favorite food:** McDonald's and chicken chow mein **Favorite color:** Dark brown **Favorite school subjects:** English and math **Favorite hymn:** "Amazing Grace" **Cool Brandy web site:** www.brandyland.com **Motto:** Remember All Things Are Possible If You Believe, Work Hard, and Never Say Never **Dream date:** Putt-putt golf! **Cars:** Lexus *and* Range Rover **Causes:** Education and the environment **Turn-on:** Playing hard to get **Curfew at age 17:** 12:30 A.M. **Last year in "normal" high school:** 9th grade **Beauty tip:** She washes her face every night **Non-profit organization:** Norwood Kids Foundation **Instrument played:** piano.